Noises in the Woods

by Judi Friedman
pictures by John Hamberger

A Fat Cat Book

E.P. Dutton   New York

Library of Congress Cataloging in Publication Data

Friedman, Judi, date   Noises in the woods.
                (A Fat cat book)

SUMMARY: Explains how to follow sounds to find forest
animals during the day and at night and identifies the
makers of some familiar sounds.
1. Forest fauna—Juvenile literature.   2. Animal sounds—
Juvenile literature.   [1. Forest animals.   2. Animal
sounds]   I. Hamberger, John.   II. Title.   III. Series.
QL112.F74   591.5'264   78-12924   ISBN: 0-525-36023-9

Published in the United States by E. P. Dutton, a Division
of Sequoia-Elsevier Publishing Company, Inc., New York

Published simultaneously in Canada by Clarke,
Irwin & Company Limited, Toronto and Vancouver

Editor: Ann Troy   Designer: Patricia Lowy
Printed in the U.S.A.   First Edition
10 9 8 7 6 5 4 3 2 1

To Jean and David,

with deepest love and gratitude

Contents

How To See Animals

Many animals live in the woods. Most of us never see them. The animals are afraid of people. They run away.

Some animals will not run away if you are very still. Try not to talk. Listen for noises. Then try to find the animal who is making the noises.

Move very slowly. Try not to walk on
sticks or dry leaves. Walk carefully so you
do not fall. Move when you hear the
noise. Stop when the noise stops. The
animal may hide if he hears you.

Some animals have eyes on the sides of their heads. They may not seem to be looking at you. However, they can still see you. Try to move when the animal's head is turned away from you.

The animal may run away if he sees you. Try not to move quickly.

An animal might run away if he smells
you. Try to smell like things that belong
in the woods. Rub yourself with something like pine needles.

Don't be afraid. When you are afraid, you give off a funny smell. Some animals will not like it. They might run away.

Animals will not hurt you when you just look at them. Do not touch wild animals. If you do, they might think that you will hurt them. They might bite you.

In the Daylight

Try going into the woods in the day-
light. You might ask someone to go with
you. Sit down and listen.

You may hear something under the
bushes. Brown leaves may fly up. Walk
slowly over to them.

The noises might sound as if they are being made by a big animal. There is nothing to be afraid of. A little head may pop out. It may be just a small bird. He eats worms. He kicks up dry leaves to find them.

There are sounds in the sky, too. Look
up! You may see some crows. They may
be flying around and around.

You might want to find out why the
crows are so noisy. Walk closer to the
sounds. A big owl may be sitting in a tree
near their nests. She eats baby crows.

Many animals live in or near water.
Rivers, ponds, and lakes are good places
to see animals. Some frogs make big,
deep noises in the summer.

Listen for the big noise of the bullfrog.
Find out where it is coming from. Look
for his yellow throat. It moves in and out
when he makes noise.

The frog will splash if he jumps into the water. Look down into the water. He may be under some plants.

In the Night

Everything seems different at night. People are not used to being in the woods in the dark. They cannot see well. But after about forty minutes outdoors, their eyes get used to the dark.

Put thin red paper over the end of a flashlight. Many animals are not scared by red light. They are scared by white light. Now you will be able to see in the dark.

Many animals move around at night. Listening for animal noises is fun in the dark.

You may hear short chirps in the grass.
"Cree—cree—cree—cree—cree—cree."
The noises are made over and over. Walk
slowly to the sound. Find the place where
the noise is coming from. Shine the flashlight on it. A little cricket may be there.
He makes sounds by rubbing his wings
together.

Noises may come from the tops of dark trees, too. "Tseet. Tseet. Tseet." It may sound as if little birds are calling. But most birds sleep at night.

Try to make the noises. Something might call back to you. It may be a flying squirrel who lives in a tree.

Animals make lots of noises in the
water at night. Sometimes you can hear
splashing. It sounds as if someone is
taking a bath. It could be a mother
raccoon. She might be showing her
babies how to hunt for food in the water.

She may growl. A big male raccoon
might have come too near her children.

Scary Noises

Some noises sound very scary at night. Find out what is making the noises. Then they will not seem as scary.

One spooky noise sounds like an old witch. She seems to say "Oh-o-o-o-o." Follow that sound if you want to. Be careful. Don't get lost in the woods.

You may find a little owl sitting on a tree branch. He may be only as big as your head. He is making that scary noise.

It is fun to sit near a lake. You may
hear a slap on the water. That noise is
made by a big beaver. He hits his tail on
the water.

Some night you may hear a big crack-ing noise. It might have been made by a deer. She was running through the woods. She broke a dry stick. Go to the sound. The deer will be gone. Use your flashlight. You may see her tracks on the ground.

Sometimes there are creaking noises in the woods. They sound very scary. They sound like a door opening in an old, broken-down house. Find the noises. Look up! This noise is not made by an animal. It is just two tall trees. They push against each other when the wind blows.

Guess Who?

Spring is a good time of year to listen for noises. Many animals are looking for mates. Other animals have new babies to take care of. They are all looking for food after the long winter.

Try sitting outside on a spring night.

Sit in the woods near a pond or a lake.

You may hear these sounds.

"Splash! Splish, splash."

"Cree—cree—cree—cree—cree—cree."

"Tseet. Tseet. Tseet."

"Grrrrrrr-rrr."

"Oh-o-o-o-o."

"SLAP!"

"CRACK!"

"Creeeeeeeeeeeak."

Guess what is making those noises!

"Splash! Splish, splash."   Frog

"Cree—cree—cree—"   Cricket

"Tseet. Tseet. Tseet."   Flying squirrel

"Grrrrrrr-rrr."   Raccoon

"Oh-o-o-o-o-"   Owl

"SLAP!"   Beaver

"CRACK!"   Deer

"Creeeeeeeeeeeeak."   Trees